ESCAPE FROM THE DARK PRINCE

The Adventures of Johnny McGinnis

Written By:

Mickey Wilcox

June, 2013

CONTENTS

Author's Forward

I wrote this book in the hopes that it would capture people's imagination and incite within them a desire to seize the adventures in the world that are there for the taking. Life is meant to live, we have a world to explore, and billions of people to get to know and create life-long friendships with. I think there are few things sadder than a man or woman that has grown old and reflects back on their life and realizes that they let it pass them by, never to have that time again.

God gave us a wonderful opportunity, but it is only for those who are willing to grab ahold of it. There is greatness in each of us. We are made that way. All you have to do is put your hand in the hand of God and walk with Him to that greatness. On that path you will find your destiny and your greatness. The world will be a greater place because you walked that path. Your children and grandchildren will have someone that they will look to and follow into greatness themselves.

Although I write this with my son's age group in mind, that being pre-teen and teen, I believe it to be a book that can inspire and encourage everyone. It is never too late to step into the greatness of your destiny.

Every adventure that our character finds himself in is based on a real life adventure. The circumstances and people are different, and our main character is fictitious. However, the adventures are from people I know, or have read about, or are from my own life.

May God bless you as you read this and may something in your soul be stirred to inspire you to reach for the greatness God has for you.

Mickey Wilcox

ASK OF ME, AND I WILL MAKE THE NATIONS YOUR HERITAGE, AND THE ENDS OF THE EARTH YOUR POSSESSION.

PSALM 2:8

CHAPTER 1

RUN FOR YOUR LIFE!

Once again I, Johnny McGinnis, found myself lying face down in the mud trying to hide from my pursuers. This time they almost got me. It was a close call. The lookout came rushing inside yelling "Run"! No sooner did he get that single word out, then the door behind him exploded and he disappeared in a blinding mix of smoke and sound. There was chaos as black-clad, machine gun carrying soldiers rushed through the door. My interpreter and friend, Dr. Ho, grabbed me by the arm and rushed me out a secret back door directly behind where I was standing. To be honest, it was less of a door and more of a poorly patched section of back wall. It was here for just such an occasion. We ran into the blackness of the night as the other one hundred plus men and women did. We all knew the risk in meeting. Many of them had already been to prison or even tortured. But it was worth it. We each had committed our lives to doing what is right and living with honor rather than cowering in fear. We knew the truth and by knowing it, we had to make a decision.

Now my decision had left my friend and I lying in the mud, in this freezing, rain soaked mountainside. Already my fingers were growing numb with the cold. My outer clothes were wet and it was just a matter of time before the wet penetrated to my skin. This was going to be a long cold night. I sure hoped I wouldn't freeze to death. Ha! Wouldn't that be something? I escape the storm troopers working for the Dark Prince only to die from exposure. Well, at least they wouldn't get to torture me that way. I know some day I will get caught and they will probably torture me, but to be honest, it scares me. I have friends all over the world who have survived being tortured and the things they have shared with me are brutal. Those that work for the Dark Prince can come up with some very disturbing and painful things. They make an art of inflicting as much pain as possible, while still keeping you alive. They are skilled artists, if you could call it an art.

We crawled along this ditch we were in periodically lifting our heads to see how far away from the troops we were. Every once in a while we would catch a glimpse of another brother or sister from the secret meeting sliding over a large rock or crouching to run across the one lane road. In twos and threes they would move. As far as I could tell, no one seemed to have gotten caught. The storm troopers, whoever they were, still kept up a search. In the ever widening distance behind us I could see flashlight beams going everywhere, but none focused for long and none grouped together in one spot. These would have been the signs that someone had gotten caught. Most of the yelling had died down long ago. Now the storm troopers seemed to go about quietly and intently searching the rocky land surrounding the building we had been meeting in.

A truck had since pulled up after we fled. We heard it as we were first dodging along rocks and ditches. Their troops had snuck up and organized for the suddenness of the raid. They got past our lookout, so they must have been good. These were not local police or local militia. They were specialty troops. The way they worked together, the stealth in their arrival, and the equipment they carried all said the same thing: highly trained government troops. That's the way it is. In some parts of the world, like where I come from, governments don't yet work for the Dark Prince; although that has been changing as of late. Here it was a different story; the government was used by the Dark Prince to hunt us down. Their job was to capture us and interrogate us to find out where the rest of our people were hiding. They wanted to know who the kingdom people were. And how do we communicate with one another? Already there were record numbers of kingdom people in prison here. They wouldn't kill us right now if they could avoid it. They still worried about world opinion towards their country.

Our rules for this meeting were pretty simple. Come only in groups of two or three. Do not drive, which was easy because most of the kingdom leaders here do not own cars. Come at night. Dress warm and be prepared for the unexpected. That was it, the rule book for the meeting.

It was pretty humbling for me actually. They came to see me and hear what I had to say. All I could think was, what can I tell these men and women? They had all faced worse than me, and they survived in a hostile land. Most, if not all, had been in prison and tortured. They all wore rags for clothes and had next to no meat on their bones. They lived in poverty and were hunted like animals.

When my friend Dr. Ho asked me to come and speak with them, he explained that it would be dangerous, but that it would encourage them and give them strength to keep working hard for the kingdom. How could I say no? Whatever I could do to help was what I had told my friend. We had parked our car at a trusted brother's house in a nearby town and set off by foot from there. It was a silent walk out of the town and into the rocky wilderness surrounding the town. We walked for a couple hours. We traveled slower than I would have on my own. I don't know if Dr. Ho was going slow thinking that it would be hard for me to keep up or if it was difficult for him. Now, looking back, I think he may have gone slowly so that I could get a feel for how to get back on my own. Had he been shot or captured, it would leave me on my own to find my way back.

When we arrived at the old building for our meeting, I was surprised to see that there were no windows and no stove to keep us warm. There was only a front door. It was a single story, mainly wood building barely big enough to hold all of us. It was unobtrusive and really didn't stand out much in its rocky outcropped surroundings.

After getting there, we shook hands with a few of the other brothers and sisters that were already there. Nobody spoke much and it seemed rather quiet. I began to think that this was going to be a long boring night. I resigned myself to the thought that at least I can encourage them and it was a nice walk out here.

As we sat in relative silence waiting for the rest of the men and women to show up, I tried to learn as much about them as possible by the way they looked. All of them walked strange, as if their bodies hurt. All their expressions were serious and weary. Not just a little bit tired from a long walk or a long day, but from a long hard life. I was really saddened to see them. I also noticed that for all the weariness and the apparent pains in their bodies, they all seemed to be rather at peace.

After everyone arrived, Dr. Ho stood to speak. He said a few words in Mandarin, their language that I do not understand, and then everyone stood and we began to sing quietly. After this and some prayers, I think (as I said, I couldn't understand their language) we all sat down and Dr. Ho introduced me.

I stood to speak alongside Dr. Ho who would translate for me. From the moment I stood to speak, out of the depths of my soul, there was a great pity for all of these men and woman. They had been kingdom leaders for many years, some longer than I had even been alive. Who was I to encourage them? But that wasn't the pity in my deepest parts, it was for their hurt. After spending a few minutes fumbling for the right words to say, I finally gave into the feelings of pity and turned to my friend, Dr. Ho.

"Dr. Ho," I said, "I feel it is important that I pray over someone here before I can go on. Would that be okay, and not out of order?"

He replied that it would be fine; however I felt it best to proceed. I turned back to the crowd gathered before me and began to speak. This time, instead of my prepared thoughts, I just spoke from my heart.

"Brothers and sisters," I said, "I feel God wants to do something for someone here. I feel as though there is someone here with a serious back problem and God wants to heal it. If you have a back problem, please come forward so that I might pray over it and God will heal you."

Imagine my surprise when almost everyone in the room raised their hand and came forward! I looked at Dr. Ho thinking I had done something wrong. He smiled a great big smile, one that was way too big for his tiny little frame. He said "Brother Johnny, almost all of these brothers and sisters have been in prison at least once and most of them have been tortured many times. Their backs hurt from poor diet and harsh conditions."

As I looked around at all the men and women that were coming forward for prayer, I thought about how God better do something because I sure didn't know what to do! If I thought I was under qualified at the beginning that was an understatement. But what can you do? To see God do the amazing, one has to take courage when He calls on them. So I stepped forward to meet these men and women. I laid hands on one person at a time and prayed short prayers of healing. One by one they began to shout praises! As they shouted and began dancing around, I used less and less words. I would just touch them and Bam! They were healed. It was crazy.

After I was through praying for each one of them, I began to speak words of encouragement to them and that is when everything changed. The door burst open, our lookout yelled Run! And then everything exploded. Now here I am running in the darkness and trying not to get caught by the storm troopers.

After a maddening amount of time traveling in the freezing cold and pitch blackness of night, we could begin to see the city lights ahead of us. "Just a little further" I thought to myself. So far, Dr. Ho had said almost nothing. I knew we had to be quiet, but I really had a lot of questions to ask. I had to remember that we were not yet out of a life and death run. My mind was bubbling over with thoughts and questions with no answers yet.

By now the freezing water and mud I had been lying in had worked its way to my skin. The adrenaline that I first had when we ran out of the meeting place had worn off and now I was exhausted and freezing. How did Dr. Ho do it? He had to be freezing. He was next to me in the mud, face down just like I was. I couldn't see him very well because of the darkness of the night, but I knew he had to be just as covered with mud as I was. How was he enduring this cold? True, he lived here in the northern territories of China, but he was just a small framed frail old man. He was nothing more than skin and bones. His coat was thick and made of a leathery material, but there really wasn't much to Dr. Ho's body. Maybe it was some weird Chinese mind discipline thing. I laughed out loud as I pictured him sitting cross legged under some freezing waterfall way up north somewhere.

Dr. Ho looked at me and asked, "What is so funny, my brother? Why do you laugh?"

"Nothing really brother," I said, "I was just wondering how you have managed to stay so warm while I am freezing."

He gave me a strange look like he didn't fully understand what I was asking. Then he said "my coat, brother!" and he began to laugh. He seemed to think it was the funniest thing he had ever heard. I was starting to get embarrassed when he finally stopped laughing.

"Brother," he began again, "my coat is fur lined and it is made of an oilskin. I keep it covered well in oils to keep the water out. Many times I have had to flee from the police and the military. They are always hunting us; so now I always dress so that I may run and stay warm." He smiled at me with his big yellowed smile.

With that I began to laugh with him. How could I have ever thought that a kingdom man like him would not always have to be prepared to flee? I always forget that his country is nothing at all like my country. Here the Dark Prince controls the government. That means that the police and the military are always looking for the Kingdom people.

I have been in this country now for a month working with Dr. Ho. My job is to assess the communications situation here and report how we can best implement a global communication network for the Kingdom workers. Right now we can send some emails that are coded and letters will usually get to their recipients. However, we anticipate all that becoming less likely to work in the near future as the Dark Prince gains more and more control over the whole world. We are already seeing "global" laws being passed in my own country. There have been many social changes that are making it harder for Kingdom workers to meet and work. And I am the one who lives in a free country.

I was so lost in my thoughts that Dr. Ho startled me when he grabbed my arm and whispered very firmly "get down!"

We were almost to the house where we had left our car. In front of us was a small stone wall that ran parallel to the side of the house. We ducked down behind it. Dr. Ho led the way as we belly crawled along the wall toward the front of the house. Part way there, Dr. Ho stopped and without a word began to wrestle with some stones in the wall. After a moment he began to move the stones aside revealing a secret entrance into a small low storage shed on the other side of the wall. He motioned me forward as he slithered into this small opening. Next was my turn. I could not fit through on my first attempt. My six foot tall 220 pound frame didn't fit well into Chinese secret hiding holes. I backed out on my stomach and slid my right arm in. I was lying on my side and pushed one arm and my head in. I willed my left arm down as low as possible and drew in my upper torso. After that my hips and legs went in with no problem. After I was in, it took a moment to get straightened out. There was no light in here except what came in through our secret entrance.

Dr. Ho never said a word. After I got in and situated myself parallel to his body, he simply rolled over top of me and took a position nearest the entrance. Carefully he began to place each stone back into its proper place. Now we were completely in the dark. Dr. Ho whispered to me that we would stay here until early morning. I figured that was in about an hour or two at the most.

I tried to sleep, but this evening's events kept replaying over and over again in my mind. How great is God? I wanted to stand up and shout how much I loved Him and how great He was.

He put it on my heart to pray for someone's hurt back. When I asked them to come forward, almost everyone did. I prayed for each one, and as I did, He healed each one. Had He not done that, many of our brothers and sisters in the Kingdom would never have escaped. Somehow I believed that even the lookout had made it. It really didn't make any sense. I saw him disappear in the explosion that must have been the storm troopers blowing open the door. But something inside of me told me that he was alive and had escaped. How awesome is God? I lay there singing quietly in my mind praises to God, telling Him how awesome He is and how much I loved Him.

I don't know if I had fallen asleep or if I was just so caught up in my prayers that I had completely blocked out everything else. But I was startled back to consciousness by the song of a bird. It must have landed on the roof of this small storage building we were hiding in, because it was really loud. Dr. Ho must have fallen asleep, or maybe like me, was caught up in silent worship because his small frame was startled when the bird sounded. Again, without a word, he rolled right over top of me and with his head; he lifted the roof of the small storage shed and looked outside.

He lay back down and whispered into the darkness, just loud enough for me to hear. "Brother, we must stay here. There may be a problem because our signal light has not been lit."

I laid there wondering if I was going to have to find my own way back home. We had a back-up plan for me to get out of the country, but it was not expected for me to go this far north. If I had to walk south avoiding all the police and military along the way, I would never make it back to my pick up point in time. If I missed my flight and my emergency pick up point, they would assume I was either dead or our mission had been compromised and then they would bug out. Our Kingdom ship parked off the coast in international waters could not afford to be captured or sunk; although sinking was preferred to capture. My mind suddenly began to race. I had friendly contacts in southern India that I knew really well. They were on the southwestern coast so I would have to traverse an ocean somehow. I had a friend in Cambodia I was meeting for an upcoming mission in that part of the world, but I didn't even know where in Cambodia he lived. I had an old friend in Japan, but that would mean me having to cross the entire width of China; while being hunted. I guess India would be my best course. Lord willing, things would go smooth and I wouldn't have to come up with my own escape plan. I closed my eyes and began to pray silently.

Suddenly I was blinded by a bright light. With a start my eyes popped open and I lay there frozen. As my eyes focused on the sudden intrusion of light, I saw a little Asian head with a furry cap and a set of grinning yellow teeth.

"Hello, Brother Johnny!" Sam said as friendly as could be.

It was Sam Cho, the kingdom worker who owned this house and was hiding our car.

As we climbed out of the small storage building across the yard from Sam's home, he began to apologize over and over for not lighting the "all clear" lamp.

My body didn't want to move right from lying there unmoving for so long and being cold and damp all the way through to my bones. Dr. Ho and I hobbled to the house while Sam kept chattering away; sometimes in broken English and sometimes in Mandarin. The jist of what I understood was that he wanted to look for something or someone before he came to get us.

When we got into the house, Sam stopped talking and closed and locked the door after us. Immediately his wife came in with hot tea and blankets. She took my coat and wrapped me in a blanket. Sam took both Dr. Ho and myself by the elbow and led us to a nearby couch for us to sit down on. The soft cushion and the blanket felt great. The tea was so hot and I drank it slow feeling the warmth spread throughout my body slowly.

After a short while of sitting there drinking tea, Sam explained to me that his wife had prepared a hot bath for me and set out some clothes that should fit me. I allowed his wife to lead me into an adjoining room where there was a tub with steaming water in. She pointed out the clothing and a towel, along with another pot which turned out to be filled with cold water. She then smiled and bowed as she backed out of the room.

I quickly peeled off my wet cloths and slid carefully into the almost too small tub. Ahhhh… It felt so good. I could spend hours in this tub. The water was a little too hot, but I didn't care. My body was enjoying the warmth, even if it was making my skin red.

I washed, and with reluctance, got out and dried. Dr. Ho would need a bath also, and I didn't want to be rude and make him wait any longer then he needed to. I was surprised that the clothes fit as well as they did. My thoughts were suddenly interrupted by a small knock at the door. "Come in" I said. Immediately Sam's wife entered and bowed politely. She gathered up my clothing and disappeared.

I stepped out into the adjoining room and there was Sam and Dr. Ho. They rose to greet me as I entered. I bowed slightly as seemed to be the proper response. We all took a seat as Sam's wife brought out more tea.

Dr. Ho asked how my bath felt and explained that he too would have one after Sam's wife prepared more water. "In the meantime," said Dr. Ho, "allow me to update you on what Sam and I were talking about." With that he began to explain last night's ordeal.

"We do not think that the government police knew you were there, which is a good thing. There has been no mention from our contacts about an American or European. This is good because you should still be safe to leave our country by air."

What a relief! I said a silent, yet quick prayer of thanksgiving to God. Dr. Ho continued. "As near as we can establish at this time, none of our people were captured or killed."

My mouth formed to ask about the lookout, but Dr. Ho just waved his hand and smiled. "Jing Cho is okay and will make a full recovery." said Dr. Ho. He continued, "Jing Cho, our lookout last night was found by the soldiers to be still alive in the rubble of the door. The soldiers put him in the back of their truck as a prisoner. Some of our people saw him there and God made an opportunity for them to get Jing Cho off and carry him to safety. He has some minor wounds but he will heal."

Dr. Ho continued to explain that Sam had not come to get us first thing in the morning because he wanted to check with friends to see if the military was looking for me. When he found that they were not, he returned to get us.

With that, Sam's wife entered bringing in breakfast foods and led Dr. Ho into the bath, leaving Sam and I alone. We bowed for a word of thanks to God for this food. I reached out and took a warm piece of fresh bread and put some honey on it. Wow! It tasted like the best meal I had ever had. I did not realize how hungry I was until then.

Sam began to explain today's plan to me. We would stay here and rest for most of the day. We would have an early dinner and then be off when everyone else was returning from work. This plan would allow our travels to blend in with everyone else who was traveling in the city.

I had one more week in this country before my flight leaves. This would give me an opportunity to complete my evaluation. I am thankful for last night's adventure, even if it was more than I expected. Last night put the dangers that these men and women face every day into perspective for me. These thoughts would definitely be a part of my report.

CHAPTER 2

SMUGGLING FROM CAMBODIA!

After a short flight from China to Australia, our helicopter picked me up and carried me to our Kingdom ship called *The Messenger*. It was good to be back in my own quarters again. I have only been with The Messenger crew for a year now, but already they felt like family.

The mission of The Messenger was to strengthen the relationship and communications with kingdom workers all over the world, helping to identify means of support for their local mission and bringing that support to them. We were based out of Georgia on the East coast of The United States of America. It was considered by most to be the last outpost of free Christianity. Sadly, in my day we are watching that freedom fade away. The Dark Prince was gaining strength even there. His direct influence could be seen everywhere you turned.

After a pretty good childhood, and a short tour in the military, I found myself wondering what was next. I had a pretty good job and my parents were proud of me. I had never really been in trouble. I was raised in church with a younger sister and an older brother. I wasn't ready to get married and settle down. I wanted something more, but my life was really feeling like a dead end.

One Sunday evening at church with my family, there was a guest speaker. He was sharing about a program in Georgia. He started with this, "Do you feel like there is more to life than what you've got going on? Are you physically able to walk, swim, and run? Is your heart yearning for adventure?" It was as if he was talking to me alone. I listened attentively to what he had to say. He said he had a program in central Georgia that was called Kingdom Disciples. It was an intensive "boot camp" for Christians who want more than church and life as we know it. This was a nine month intensive program that gave you an in depth understanding of the Gospel and taught you skills to survive in any condition as a missionary. After the nine month program you would be placed in a two month apprenticeship in an area of ministry that you felt led to work in. Then in the twelfth and final month you would return for debriefing, evaluation of your chosen field, and graduation.

I did boot camp in the Marines; how hard can an over glorified church camp be? I was hooked from that moment. I never thought much about ministry. True, I went to church and considered myself a Christian. I even made a profession of faith at one point in a church vacation Bible school. This program sounded pretty interesting, even if it was a church camp. At dinner that night I told my parents that I had decided to go to this Kingdom Disciple camp.

I will never forget my first day at camp. There were ten of us in our team. Men and women mixed. All of us were about the same age. Our instructor explained the rules of this first phase and then got in a boat and went to the other side of the river to wait on us. We each had a section of rope and a set of short instructions. We had to work together to build a rope bridge across this river. We would be shown where our tents and mess hall were after our entire team got across. This was crazy. I was the only one in our group from the military. The rest were college kids and church kids. They had no idea what to do or how to do it. None of them wanted to listen to me, and I sure didn't want to listen to some kids that didn't have any idea what to do. It was 9 o'clock in the morning. By 10 o'clock that night our last person made it across. None of us wanted to talk to each other. This was going to be a lot harder than I thought it was going to be.

By the end of the first month of intensive Bible drills (learning the basics of the Bible), basic teamwork building games, and basic wilderness survival, we were graduating into the second phase of our school. We only lost one girl who decided this was not for her and so she left. It was during this time that I began to discover that I had no real relationship with Jesus. I had heard all these teachings before, but they had never sunk in like they did now. Now I wasn't just a Christian in name only, I was a believer! I truly gave my life to Jesus. I began to see how my life differed from what He wanted for me. How I had lived my life to satisfy me and not Him. Before prayers were only for giving thanks at dinner and a bedtime prayer when I was a kid. As an adult I prayed when I needed a new job, or a new motorcycle, and of course, when I was in the Marines I prayed that they wouldn't kill me in boot camp! But now, my prayers were conversations with Jesus. They were less about me and more about me becoming like Him. I was sold out, and it felt great! I was glad to get on my knees and ask Him to forgive me for living for myself and not Him. I asked Him to make me His, and I promised that I would live for Him and serve Him. I felt like a new man. It was exhilarating!

After graduating from the Kingdom Disciple program, I was again faced with what to do. My apprenticeship choice was to be a Pastor. That was a failure. I hated it. I felt trapped and my future looked really bleak. I went to our camp leader to seek his advice. He suggested we fast and pray and wait on God for an answer. So we did just that. I was back at home now and he would call every day to see how it was going for me. He even came up a couple weekends to stay with me when he could. One of those weekends he came to me and told me that he had a friend that did high risk mission work on a ship called The Messenger and asked if I would be interested. I said sure and it wasn't long before a recruiter from The Messenger came to meet with me. A year later and here I am. I am a field operative, well, I should say, I am a junior field operative. After a year they let me go on a solo trip, in another six months they will evaluate my progress and either promote me to a full field operative or reassign me to a desk or support crewman. So far, things seem to be going pretty well for my promotion.

I was now back on *The Messenger*, showered and shaved and finished with my mission debrief. I had turned in my assessment and recommendations. Everyone seemed happy about what I had to say and they were praising God for the crazy things that had happened in the north.

It had been two weeks and I was getting restless. I was really looking forward to going back out in the field. It wasn't long before my desire was filled. I would be helicoptered into Cambodia to a mission center and orphanage. I would fly to the international airport where Danny Brown would pick me up and take me to the mission center. Along with me would be a cargo of 10,000 Vietnamese pocket Bibles and 500 small single station FM radios for a new underground bible teaching station. I would spend about two weeks in Cambodia helping to smuggle the Bibles into Vietnam and setting up the pirate radio station. When I left, I would meet up with some friends of the ministry and I would go with them by sailboat to the Philippines and connect with a ministry there until *The Messenger* was able to come and pick me up. She had some work to do up in the Persian Gulf and would return at her earliest convenience. It sounded great to me. I had always wanted to go to the Philippines.

It was 6 am and I was standing on the helo-pad on *The Messenger*. I had an early breakfast and a short last minute briefing in the ready room. Now I was standing here as the support crew loaded the Bibles and radio receivers, along with the mobile pirate radio transmitter.

After everything was loaded, the crew chief waved me and the mission support crew onboard. We took our seats in this modified "Huey" that had been picked up at a military surplus and refitted for our needs. As we took off, I watched our mobile home shrink into the distance. I closed my eyes and tried to imagine what it would be like to smuggle Bibles across the border. In my briefing they made sure to mention that the least that would happen if we got caught would be that I would go to prison. They didn't think that the U.S. consulate would be much help in getting me released. "Don't worry," they said, "we have friends in a lot of the prisons that will help to make it easier on you, but expect the worst. So don't get caught." What a word of encouragement that was. I had to laugh. A couple weeks ago I was freezing my butt off running for my life in northern China; now, I'm off to the jungles of south-east Asia. What a life! With that thought, I began to praise Jesus. Who could have ever thought that being a Christian could be so much fun and have so much adventure?

I was caught up in the silence of my private worship and thoughts when I was jolted back to reality as we touched down on the tarmac of the runway. I grabbed my gear and headed to immigration and security. I had to get through there first. The support crew would off-load our equipment to a customs truck and after they rummaged through it and we paid a few extortion costs they would most likely release our things and I could begin my work.

I got through all the entry things I needed to get through and Danny Brown was standing there waiting for me. He was six foot four and a giant. I thought I was big next to these Cambodians, but Danny was even bigger. I knew it was him with his sandy blond hair and deep tan, from the picture of him hanging in the ready room on The Messenger. He looked like a California surfer. He came right up to me and grabbed my hand. Pulling me into a massive bear-hug, he boomed "Johnny McGinnis! Praise God and welcome to Cambodia!" Without letting go, he said, "We are gonna have a great time."

He walked with me out to his beat up old truck and we pulled around to customs. I sat in the cab in the sweltering heat while he went in to talk to the customs officials. If I had to guess I'd say he had to pay all kinds of fees to get the equipment. It's par for the course when dealing with third world countries.

The heat was more than humid, it was oppressive. You almost couldn't breathe. After what felt like hours, Danny emerged with his massive grin displaying a perfect set of white teeth. I thought, he could be a movie star, but instead he is living in the middle of the jungle caring for orphans and smuggling Bibles. I had to laugh. I was smiling when he jumped in the truck and started it right up and swung us into the customs yard. As we were pulling in, Danny told me that they were arguing over getting some radios. "I played it real cool and told them that they were for friends of mine, but if they insisted, I would give them each one." Danny started laughing. "They took 10 of them for their children and wives." I thought he was going to never stop laughing long enough to finish telling me what had happened. "Little do they know," he continued between laughs, "they are all tuned to one station, our Pirate Gospel station!" With that, I started laughing with him. He said it also cost him $20 in American money. We backed up to a small metal building and jumped out to load up our stuff. It was all by hand and it was hot! It didn't take us long and we were off. We went back to Danny's place to unload and get me settled in.

After about two hours on alternating mud and paved roads, a sudden down pour, and even more oppressive heat, we arrived at the town Danny lived in. His non-air conditioned truck was like an oven with the stagnate heat barely moving as we drove through it. We came up to a small compound with several small buildings and a gated court-yard. None of it was really impressive, nor did it stand out among the other buildings in the town. Really, the only difference was that this court-yard was bigger and the sign over the entrance was both in English and Khmer. You could tell he was loved here. As we pulled up and honked his horn, we barely had to slow down as the kids rushed to open the gate. As we pulled in, they surrounded the truck saying all kinds of things in a mix of languages. We got stopped in front of a small windowless metal building and Danny gently pushed his way through the crowd of kids and unlocked the door to the building. He said a few words and some of the kids jumped on the truck and began to unload. They moved the things into the building while Danny walked me to what turned out to be the campus kitchen. It was a few crude picnic tables, a fire pit with a kettle and assorted pots. It was a screened-in building with a couple of ceiling fans. It was a nice respite from the staggering heat. We sat down and chatted over a couple of warm Cokes.

The next week was uneventful as I settled in and got used to the heat and humidity. I spent time with the kids and going on home visits with Danny. He pastored a small church that met 3 times a week including Sunday morning service. The rest of the time was spent administering the orphanage and associated school.

It was Monday afternoon and we were loading up a small river boat with the Bibles and the radios. We were off to smuggle them into Vietnam. We would do it by water because there was less security. According to Danny, they didn't have the resources to stop every boat so they only stopped random boats. He said that he gets stopped about half the time because he was an American, but he had been traveling the river so much that they never looked too closely at his cargo.

The boat was a small river boat common to this area. It looked like every other river boat on the water. It had a center roof for the cargo area and a long pointed prowl. The engine was of a kind that was on a long shaft with a two stroke motor on one end and a flat mounted propeller on the other. Danny stood at the back of the boat, or the aft end as boaters liked to call it, and I sat down low next to the cargo. I was big and white and didn't want to draw any more attention to us than was necessary. We also had an old Montyard mountain villager with us named Charlie. Charlie used to be mercenary before he gave his life to Jesus. He still had a strong look about him. He didn't seem like the kind of man you wanted to mess around with. He didn't speak very much English, but he managed to get his point across. It was his boat we were on. He and Danny used it to carry supplies for the poor into Vietnam, and bring needed supplies back up to Cambodia. By doing this it made it easier to smuggle Bibles. Normally they only carried a small amount of Bibles, but the demand was growing so much that they had to risk bringing in larger shipments. That is what gave them the idea of a pirate radio station. They would pass out small handheld solar powered radios, which came preset on one radio frequency. The transmitter would be given to a kingdom contact in Vietnam who would hide it in a vehicle; a car, or a van, or a truck. It was completely portable and self-contained. There were two wires, called power leads that were run to the vehicles battery to power the unit. Also, there was a module that was screwed into the metal body of the car or van that allowed the vehicle body to act as the transmitting antenna. In this way the whole transmitting unit could be moved from place to place to avoid detection. A person could change vehicles in a hurry or drive from place to place. We could switch users, locations, or a variety of different strategies to keep our Bible teachings and Kingdom messages on the air.

This one was actually a test package. We were trying to streamline it and make it as effective as possible. Although publicly Vietnam was open to free choice in religion, it was well documented and well known in the country that to be a part of the Kingdom meant imprisonment and even death. This was an ideal place to test this equipment. Vietnam is continually damp and humid. Primitive conditions and crude roads; a hostile government and a strong desire by the people to know the freedom that the Kingdom brings made it a perfect place to tweak our equipment and make it easier to be mainstreamed into kingdom use.

The Dark Prince had a firm grip on the government here. Death squads in neighboring countries frequently spilled over into Vietnam. The government itself usually knew that these things would happen but turned a blind eye to it. Not only that, but when they would find out about a group of kingdom people meeting together, they would raid it, sometimes massacring everyone they found. Men, women, children, entire families; it made no difference to them. That is how the Dark Prince operated. He convinced people that they had to be brutal in their efforts to stop the kingdom. Religion was a big part of his strategy. He had no one religion, he had created thousands of them. He allows people to make up their own religion, often encouraging it. But in the end he focuses their hate towards the Kingdom and then ultimately he will laugh while destroying his own followers. Its madness, but that is the way he operates and people fall for it over and over.

As we traveled lazily down the river with the constant whine of the two stroke outboard, I looked around at the beautiful scenery. Lush and green jungle surrounded both sides of the river. The boat swayed gently in the muddy river. There were many boats that went up and down the river as this was a major artery for supplies.

Every once in a while we would see an old military style PT boat. They were a fast plywood boat with a forward mounted machine gun. On the roof was a light and siren and on board were about a half dozen armed soldiers. As we got closer to the border, the more we saw.

We entered an area well populated with river traffic and large river ports on each side of the river. This was the border between both countries. As we crossed over, we didn't alter our direction or speed. Danny said in a tone a little louder than a whisper so that I could hear over the drone of the motor that we had crossed the border. "Pray," He said, "we don't want to get stopped and searched right now."

The Montyard and I closed our eyes and began a silent prayer. After I prayed, I opened my eyes and saw us moving gently forward towards our destination. We passed several boats as we came upon a large slow bend in the river. You could see a sliver of an island through the peak of the bend. On it was a large dock with many boats and what appeared to be lots of armed soldiers. Danny whispered that it was the border police. You could feel the tension on our boat as we slid past. We tried to blend in to the dozen or so boats around us headed the same way.

So far so good, I thought to myself. I tried not to look at the police dock. I remembered my old Marine Corps training; when hiding behind a tree, think that you are the tree. I really don't know how well that worked, but I do know that if you focus your mind on a man you're trying to sneak up on, something alarms them and they will turn around on you. Better safe than sorry. We were nearly past them and out of sight. The heat was oppressive. The bugs were annoying. I have no idea how the Montyard was able to keep from swatting them. My heart skipped a beat when suddenly, from the dock, we heard a siren. Within moments a police boat came racing up beside us. I had no idea what to do as these armed men came towards us. All I could do was stare blankly at them and avoid the impulse to jump in the river and try to get away. Danny began to veer off to the shore on our right. As the police boat raced passed us it threw up great swells of water that threatened to roll us over. My heart started beating again. False alarm, they were not coming for us. I let out a great sigh of relief. I didn't realize it until just this moment, but I had been holding my breath. It felt good to breathe again.

Danny began to swing the boat back out into the main channel when we heard another police siren and the revving up of the big inboard motor. We couldn't see the dock any more at the border, but there was no mistaking the sound of that big-block inboard motor. Again Danny began to swing our little boat near to the shore. In no time at all we could tell that the police boat was headed right for us. We were only about fifteen minutes from our destination.   If it was us they were after it would be pointless to try and outrun them. We wouldn't make it a hundred feet. Anyway, they would probably be more than happy to open fire with that big browning M-2 .50 caliber machinegun on this little boat that held two Americans. They came close like the other boat did, but this time we heard something yelled out over a bull horn. I didn't know what they said, but I sure understood it. They wanted us to stop so they could check our cargo.

It was nerve racking to look down that big fore mounted machine gun as it was coming towards us. I began to pray, "Lord, you know that this work is for your Kingdom. Help us to come safely through this, give us strength to endure whatever will happen next. Amen"

The big police boat cut its engines down to an idle and swerved parallel to us and came along-side us all at the same time. Immediately, two armed men stood on the side of their boat pointing AK-47 assault rifles at us. Another man hurriedly tied a line from our boat to theirs. Then a uniformed man carrying a pistol boarded our boat. He looked to be the senior officer among the boats police crew. The Montyard met him face to face. They were arguing with heated words. I looked at Danny who used a down-turned hand and signaled me to stay calm. After several very tense moments where I was sure we would all be shot at any moment, our Montyard turned to Danny and said that we had to open one of our sealed packages.

Our Bibles were all in boxes of about 25 each. Each box was vacuum sealed to keep out the moisture. We had labels made for them that said they were food boxes. Our cover story was that we were bringing needed food supplies to a nearby city's homeless shelter. As soon as we opened one, they would find out quickly that the food they contained was for the spirit and not the body. We were now in a lot of trouble. The police boat stopped us on a routine drug search, as this was a major drug trafficking route. Getting caught with all these Bibles would be considered worse than drugs. The

Dark Prince had no mercy; he didn't even know what that word meant. We would, at the very least be thrown into prison. More than likely we would be tortured. If we lived through that, we would live out what was left of our lives in a Vietnamese prison camp. And they are not known for their accommodations.

With the police officer standing next to Danny, he prepared to open a sealed box marked "Food Supplies, Emergency". I knew that what would come next would be a very difficult thing for each of us standing here, but we were all Kingdom soldiers. This was always a possibility in our life. I would be mourned on board *The Messenger*, my picture would go up on the wall of martyrs if I died here. If I survived, there would be other Kingdom people who would try to do all they could to make my stay in this Vietnamese prison as endurable as possible.

Suddenly, one of the river boats came too close to us and had to swerve quickly to avoid hitting us. Its wake crashed our small boat into the big police boat. Even the men guarding us on the police boat had to grab ahold of something to keep from being knocked over. I didn't see exactly what happened with Danny, but when I recovered my balance, he was gripping his arm with his left hand. Blood was everywhere. He had dropped the box opener he was using to open the sealed boxes. The police officer with the pistol started shouting something at the Montyard and leapt back into his own boat. The police boat cast off our lines and sped away.

The Montyard reached under a seat near to him and pulled out a first aid kit. He tossed it to me and quickly took the helm. In just seconds he had us underway again to our destination. Danny and I sat with our backs against our precious cargo as I tended to his wound.

Danny looked at me with a painful grin. "God is so good," He said. "I thought for sure that we would all be going to prison today. All I could think of was how much I would miss my two sons and my wife."

I was opening a packet of chemical that would help to clot the blood and stop the bleeding. His wound didn't appear to be real deep, but it would require stiches. The best I could do was work on getting the bleeding stopped and wrap it with a large bandage.

Danny kept talking as I was working. "God always knows just when to show up," he said. "I was just about to cut open that box when that wave hit us. It made me slip and slice my arm open with my box cutter. That police captain panicked at the sight of the blood gushing from my arm. He was afraid that I would blame it on him. He told us to hurry and go to the hospital." Danny started laughing, and then I started laughing. It felt good to laugh after believing I was surly going to prison and then to escape. God is good all the time!

CHAPTER 3

ON THE RUN IN THE JUNGLE!

We made it to the city dock where we met up with some other men that would carry us and our life-saving cargo to its destination. The radios would move farther on and we would accompany them to teach the locals how to use them. Some brothers in the Kingdom off-loaded the Bibles into one truck and helped us load our radios and equipment into a car that was waiting there for us. Our car would take us to a nearby clinic so Danny could get his forearm looked at and stitched up. We were then off to our hotel room for a night to rest up before we set out to the rural area to distribute the radios and transmitter equipment.

We spent hours at the clinic waiting for our turn. There was air conditioning, but I'm not sure it was working correctly. It really didn't feel much cooler inside than outside. After the seemingly endless line of patients, Danny was finally seen. The doctor spent 10 minutes sewing him up and charged us fifty American dollars. The price was really steep, but it happens a lot when you look like an American in a third world country. Everyone thinks you're made of money. By the time we got out of there, it was nearly midnight and our arrival at our hotel was a welcomed sight.

We had decided to wait an extra day before heading out with the radios and equipment. We were taking off-road motorcycles to our destination and Danny was in a lot of pain from his stiches.

It was hot even before the sun came up. Previous arrangements had been made and two 175 trail bikes had been delivered to the hotel for us. They each had an oversized fuel tank allowing them to carry twice the fuel.

Normally they had a 2.1 gallon tank. These had a 4.5 gallon tank allowing them to travel more than 300 miles on one tank. Also they were tube tires instead of tubeless and each had a small but well stocked tool kit. They were geared differently than an American motorcycle. They sacrificed speed for power. They probably would go about 60 mph with me on the bike on a smooth level road. The difference was that they could pull me very effectively straight up a steep and rugged incline. In the jungle terrain where we were headed, this is what we would need.

A helmet was required here so each came with a nice full face helmet. Waiting at the front desk were a pair of good riding gloves and goggles.

Danny was dressed in his customary cargo shorts, tee-shirt and sandals. I was in cargo shorts, a light-weight button down shirt, my safari vest that had lots of pockets, and my bush hat that I wore everywhere I went. I also wore jungle boots. I don't know if it was my Boy Scout training to "Always Be Prepared" or my Marine Corps training, but I was a fanatic about always carrying some "just in case" things. Many people laughed at me for over packing. Why would you carry a compass and fire striker with you? They would ask me laughing. I always replied with the same answers, "I might need them." It didn't bother me. They were always happy when I had the tool or a do-dad that was needed. It is amazing how useful a simple good all-tool can be.

The radio receivers were small, about one inch thick by three inches wide, by four inches tall. They weighed only ounces. This allowed us to carry them in two modest sized backpacks. I also carried the FM transmitter. It was the size of a large book. It was about three inches thick, six inches wide, and nine inches long. It was in a shock resistant, water resistant case. There was a small head mounted microphone that plugged into the unit much like one would plug into any laptop computer. This whole transmitter weighed only about two pounds. It is amazing what we can build nowadays.

Danny and I looked over our motorcycles and checked all of our equipment. Then we knelt together for a quick word of prayer, thanking God for this day and all the blessings He has bestowed on us, and we asked Him to guide us as we went about His kingdom work today. With that we kick started our trail bikes and sped off towards our destination.

We got to the outskirts of the city and stopped at what appeared to be the only gas station around. We topped off our fuel tanks and bought a couple of bottles of water each for our trip into the jungle to our remote village where we would pass out the receivers and train the pirate radio crew. As we were in the small retail shop paying for the waters I noticed a small Vietnamese man signaling Danny. After we were paid up we went outside and pushed the motorcycles around the side of the building. There the Vietnamese man was waiting for us. He and Danny spoke for a few minutes and the man got on a small motorcycle and left. Danny came back to give me the news.

"The Bibles we brought in have been found." He said grimly. "The police raided the shop we had set up as our distribution hub. Half the Bibles had been distributed before they raided. That's the good news. The bad news is, they killed at least three people and injured several others in the raid. Nearly our entire network here has been captured and those that have not, are wanted, including the two of us. The police

55

have our descriptions and photographs. The brothers think it is best if we return to Cambodia as quickly as possible. They are worried that if we get caught it will expose our entire operation. There are only four of us that know the entire operation; me, the man we were just speaking to, and two others, the man and woman who were killed during the raid. With you Johnny, they can tie this all back to the Messenger program. This has just turned into the worst case scenario." Danny looked dead serious as he stopped talking and stared at me. "How do you think we should proceed?" he asked with a poker face.

I thought about all that he just told me. "We are here to do a job for our King, we are Kingdom men, let's do the job." "Good!" Danny replied, "I was hoping you would think that way." With that we knelt down beside our motorcycles. We began to pray and worship the most high Jesus. We thanked Him for this opportunity to serve Him and His Kingdom. We asked for courage that if we were privileged to attain the highest crown of service and be martyred for His name that we would be filled with courage.

To say these things and to pray for courage may sound strange to some, but we were Kingdom men. We were men who gave our life completely to Jesus to live and die by His ways. We were not foolish men who would race into a fire and burn to death for the sake of martyrdom. Instead, we knew that this life was only a passing time and that death was not our final destination. All people would go and stand before a most Holy God when they died here on Earth and only those who had accepted Jesus as their Lord would enter into His heaven. All others would be condemned to spend forever, that incomprehensible eternity, in Hell. Forever separated by the warmth and love of the loving God. For those of us who are redeemed by the salvation freely offered by Jesus, we do not need to fear death. For us, death is just a door to walk through into eternal life. It is only those who do not live with Jesus as their savior that must fear death, because for them, it becomes a sealed tomb of eternal death.

After our prayer and worship we fired up our motorcycles and raced off towards the jungle. It wasn't long before we ran out of good road from the city and were on a dirt and mud road. The houses became fewer and fewer. I couldn't help but notice the beauty of the jungle as we raced up the road as fast as the bikes would carry us. As we passed a small village, Danny began to slow his bike. We road side by side at only about 10 miles per hour; when Danny yelled over to me that in about five miles there would be a normal police check point. Ahead just a few miles was a foot path that led off to the south and traveled several miles through the jungle and came back north to intersect with the road on the other side of the road block. We would follow that path, but we would have to push the motor bikes so that we didn't risk alarming the police.

It was just a few minutes before Danny cut off his bike and swerved to the side of the road. He dropped the kick stand and knelt down on the jungle side of the bike and acted like he was working on something. I pulled in right behind him and did the same thing. When I went to remove my helmet he stopped me and said "leave it on for now." It didn't take long for the oppressive heat and humidity to make it hard to breath in that helmet.

We heard the rumbling high pitched sound of a large covered truck coming our way. I could feel Danny tense up as I wondered what was going on. I saw the canvas covered army truck pass us in a blur. It billowed clouds of dirt and dust behind it. I said to Danny, "How did you know?" He answered, "The Holy Spirit just spoke to me and told me that they were right behind us."

King Jesus taught us that when He went to heaven to prepare us a place there, that God the Father would send His Holy Spirit to us to guide us and be our counselor. In our line of business, we needed to always be listening to His direction. It sometimes meant life or death for us.

As soon as the truck was out of sight, we pushed the bikes off the road onto the barely discernible jungle trail. As soon as we could no longer see the road I took my helmet and goggles off. It was sweltering hot in the jungle. No air moved and the humidity was so thick that you had to push to get through it. For the next three hours we pushed our motorcycles. It was difficult work in this brutal heat. There were often times that we would have to work together to lift our bikes over fallen trees. We had to always be on the lookout for snakes. Just a little after lunch time, we finally heard the sparse traffic from the road again. We began to move more cautiously as we neared the roadway. When we could finally see it, we stopped and parked the motorcycles. I lay on my stomach and crawled out so that I could get a better look at the situation. As I cleared the brush; I could see a police road-block a little better than 100 feet west of us. We needed to go east, but there was no way that we could come out of the jungle without being noticed and get away. I could see the truck that had passed us when we first turned off into the jungle. There were two very fast looking police bikes and probably a dozen armed police officers. Each appeared to have an AK-47 machine gun. This was not looking good for us. We might outrun the motorcycles, but not the bullets. That might work in the movies, but I wasn't going to risk it in real life if I could avoid it. I slid back into the jungle to brief Danny. He studied the map. There was a branch of the jungle path that would have brought us out sooner onto the road. That would have put us out right in front of the roadblock. That meant that they must have anticipated us using the jungle path. "Somehow they know our plan," Danny said. "That means that they probably know the area that the radios are being delivered. We are going to need Gods help to get these to where they need to be."

We did what every good Kingdom man does when the odds are against them. We prayed. We remember the words of the Bible and the truths that are in it and we speak them back to God. Not really to remind Him as if He forgot, but to encourage ourselves and to cry out for God to defend us. All through-out the Bible we see recorded history of God doing amazing things to enable His people to overcome inescapable circumstances.

After our prayers we sat and waited on God and the directions of His Holy Spirit. I have read about God confusing the enemy and allowing His servants to walk past undetected. I figured God would do something like that. Almost without warning, the sky darkened. Danny looked at me and said, "You better brace yourself, it looks like a bad storm is going to blow in."

I looked up in the sky and sure enough there were really dark low hanging clouds rolling in. You could see the flashing of lightning in them. Quickly the air became electrified and the wind started blowing violently. I thought to myself "O Lord, do we really need this now? Aren't things difficult enough for us?" Suddenly the words "Escape Plan" popped into my mind. I started to laugh. Danny was moving his motorcycle under a tree when I yelled to him as quietly as possible; "Don't worry about trying to stay dry brother; this is the Lord's deliverance!" I was still laughing as Danny looked at me as if he didn't fully understand what I was saying. Then he burst out with laughter. "Halleluiah" he shouted as a massive thunder clap resounded. After putting on our helmets and fixing our goggles good and snug, we both mounted our motorcycles and fired them up. As the thunder became increasingly violent we both revved up our bikes and burst through the jungle undergrowth; first Danny then myself. The rain was coming down so hard you could barely see anything at all. I am not sure it would have mattered if we were dressed in florescent orange with a sign that said that we were the ones you are looking for. The guards appeared to be missing. They were probably huddled inside the back of the truck under the canvas tarp that covered it. As we raced up the road, I couldn't help but remember my favorite program as a young man "The Lone Ranger". As if I had no choice I pulled on the handlebars and threw myself backwards doing a wheelie on my motorcycle and shouted "Hi Ho Silver, AWAY!" I laughed so hard I almost wrecked my motorcycle. I was singing praises to God as we sped away up the muddy road.

God delivers His people in strange ways sometimes. Had we not been listening for Gods direction through His Holy Spirit, we would have been soaked, miserable, and still trying to get away from the police at the roadblock. Instead, we were laughing and singing, almost oblivious to the torrential downpour as we were getting away. Sometimes life is all about perspective. This didn't mean that everything was peaches and cream. No, on the contrary, the wind was a constant struggle for our light weight motorcycles. The raindrops were like thousands of little steel needles on our exposed skin. The mud made handling the bikes in this wind very difficult. Fish-tailing was a common experience. Even though the goggles were fog proof, the terrible humidity still made them fog up. But it was these same difficulties that were allowing us to escape and were prohibiting the enemy from pursuing us. We had not gone even five miles when the rain began to subside. What a blessing from God that storm was.

After navigating the roads for several hours, we noticed that there were frequent low flying helicopters. Danny yelled over to me as he backed off a little on his throttle allowing him to come along side of me; "I think they are looking for us. They must be pretty angry at us." We pulled off the road to come up with a new travel plan. We hid ourselves off the edge of the road and under the canopy of the jungle to look at the maps and strategize. Danny showed me where a series of old foot paths were roughly located on the map. They would take us within one mile of the village that we were headed for. We could hide the motorcycles and walk that mile. Then we would lay low until we saw our contact or a friendly, another kingdom worker, and get his attention. We could send a message to meet in a new location to distribute the radios and show the crew how to operate the radio transmitter. This sounded like a pretty good plan so we headed up the road looking for our turn off through the jungle.

We were having trouble finding the turn off because of the jungle growth. We passed where we thought it should be, so we turned around and found a place to pull off and hide the bikes. I stayed with our motorcycles while Danny went into the jungle to scout out and locate the trail. It was about forty-five minutes before he returned.

Night was about two hours away and we would need to get deep enough into the jungle so that we could minimize the risk of us being found out. It was slow going on the trail. The knobby tires dug into the soft moist dirt of the jungle floor. We moved slowly as we dodged the large plant growth and the fallen trees. Occasionally the jungle would open up and we could make really good time as we wound up the rpm's on these small but powerful dirt bikes. It was at one of these clearings that we decided that we needed to make camp before night fell and we would not be able to see any longer. We ran the bikes wide open until we came to the other side of the clearing, then we shut them down. Dismounting from our motorcycles, we came around front of each one, and grasping them by the handle-bars, we pushed them backwards. We followed back across the same trail where we first came in through the clearing. We did this in case our pursuers realized that we had gone into the jungle on this trail and they would also think that we crossed this clearing and went on.

Meanwhile, after moving backward to the point where the clearing first opened up, we located a good concealment spot a short distance off the trail. We camouflaged the motorcycles using jungle brush that we cut down from the surrounding area near our hiding spot. Then Danny and I retired to our hidden nest for the night. Danny's arm was swollen and getting red around the edges of his recently stitched-up wound. I reached in my bag and pulled out some anti-inflammatory aspirin and some topical antibiotic cream. The doctor who repaired his wrist had given him some pain medicine, but Danny was afraid that the powerful pain killer would take away his edge and cause him to react slowly. He decided to take only half of one of those pain killers tonight. Hopefully that wouldn't make him sleep too soundly, but it would take the edge off the pain.

For a man on the run and hiding in the jungle, sleeping on the bare ground, I slept very well. That is until something woke me up. Was it a sound? Maybe just an animal, or was it the police coming up the trail? I tried to quietly rouse Danny but he didn't move. The night was black tonight and you couldn't see anything. I had no idea what time it was. I dared not hit the illumination button on my watch for fear of giving away our position.

There, ahead in the distance, up near the trail, I could see a beam of light sweeping back and forth through the jungle. Their voices were muffled as they walked along the trail apparently searching for where we were located. I saw the light beams all focus together on the ground in the clearing. After what felt like forever they all switched off except one. Then they all seemed to move quickly across the clearing following the trail we had left them. Had our ruse worked? It was too early to tell, but it looked as though it had. Praise God. I said a short and quiet prayer of thanks to God and asked him to continue to keep us hidden from our pursuers.

As dawn broke I realized that I had fallen asleep again. I couldn't remember when I fell asleep. All I knew was that my body was stiff and tired. I felt worse now than when we had first laid down to sleep. It took some effort but Danny woke up. He didn't look well at all. Some of the swelling had gone down in his arm, but he looked and felt feverish. I gave him three more anti-inflammatory aspirin which he washed down with the last of his water supply. He needed good rest, food, and water. His wound needed cleaning out again.

We moved slowly as we roused ourselves and prepared to face this day God had given us. We each had our own personal pocket Bibles, so we opened them up and had a short devotional time. We took turns reading from Psalms, the book of poetry as some like to call it. It always amazes me that when I read Psalms I find words that comfort me and encourage me. David suffered so many things and often he too was being hunted down like an animal. After our short devotional time, we knelt together and prayed. We thanked the Lord for this day and asked for Him to again deliver us from the hand of the Dark Prince and his agents. We prayed for healing for Danny's forearm and safe travels up the trail to our destination. As we began to rise and get our motorcycles uncovered, we heard the whine of several motorcycles in the jungle. We stopped what we were doing and immediately dropped to the ground so we wouldn't be seen. Three motorcycles went past. They were running combat style with a driver and gunner. The gunners were carrying AK-47 machine guns that fired a 7.62 bullet. They were not as accurate as the American M-16 but the round had more umph behind it for jungle combat. If we were hit by this, it was gonna hurt, if we lived.

We had no weapons like that. As Kingdom men, we fought with different weapons. We stood on truth and that truth was carried with love. It may not sound powerful to those who do not know Jesus, or believers who have never witnessed it in action, but this weapon crushed enemy strongholds and it destroys any argument that stands opposed to God. If you still don't believe in the power of our weapon, then ask yourself why the Dark Prince would expend so much effort to hunt down a couple guys passing out simple radios to share the truth of God's word!

The Dark Prince hates Jesus and His Kingdom and everyone in it. He would rather see all men doomed to spend eternity separated from all hope and joy and love. Man was not created for the misery that life loves to give us; it is all a part of the curse of rebellion against a Holy God in this world. The Dark Prince longs to see all men destroyed and is so determined to reach that end that he will hunt down, torture, imprison, and do every kind of vial thing imaginable to accomplish his terrible scheme. He can be subtle, as he is most often, or he can be bold, as he is right now in his hunting of Danny and me.

After seeing the motorcycle gun crews go past us, we elected to go the rest of the trip by foot. If we trail-blazed our way through the jungle, we should only be about three miles away from the village. It worked out well for us being on foot and traveling cross country through the jungle. Danny's arm would have a hard time on the throttle of the motorcycle. Also the terrain was getting increasingly more difficult. As we navigated our way through the jungle carefully, we could hear the motorcycles crossing back and forth behind us on the trail.

We were about a half mile from the outskirts of the village when suddenly we heard a voice trying to get our attention in Vietnamese. I ducked down but Danny whispered back in Vietnamese. He grabbed my arm to guide me to meet the voice.

There, in a hide-out were three other men. It was cramped but it worked. It was a dug out bunker with tunnels leading off in three different directions. It was all timber reinforced walls with logs laid over for the ceiling. Over top of that was sod and natural jungle growth. There appeared to be a metallic ceiling over the logs. I asked about the strange ceiling material. It was explained to me that it was a foil blanket that doubled as a water guard and a reflector. It prevented the aerial imaging devices from finding them due to body heat while they were in the hide-out.

They explained to us that the man who warned us had been captured and tortured. They came to this village thinking that we would be here soon and they could intercept us. They also raided the home church and took the pastor and his family away. All in all, up to this point we have lost more than two dozen kingdom workers. The good news is that the radio transmission crew was right here in the bunker style hide-out. These three men had escaped the fate of the rest because this bunker was developed as a safe house for the senior kingdom workers in this village. When the Dark Prince's forces picked up the pastor and his family it tipped off the underground radio crew. The downside is that this hide-out can only be temporary. The Pastor knows to do his best to hold out for 24 hours. Odds are he will not hold out that long. He was picked up just under ten hours ago, so we were on the clock and it was ticking down.

We had a discussion on what we would do. Danny needed medical attention and to return to Cambodia. I would need to return to Cambodia and make my way down to my pick-up point with the waiting sailboat. These men needed to learn to use the transmitter and we still needed a distribution plan for the solar powered radios. Also, we had two motorcycles still stashed in the jungle that needed to be picked up. There were a lot of loose ends that needed to be worked out before we could get out of the country; all of this while we are being hunted.

We decided that the first thing would be that two of our friends would get a local medical doctor that could be trusted to come and look at Danny's arm that seemed to be getting really infected. He was also burning up with fever. While they were out they would gather up some food and supplies that we needed an do some recon to determine how aggressively the Dark Prince's forces were looking for all of us.

CHAPTER 4

ESCAPE THE LOOMING DEATH!

While the two brothers were gone, the third brother and I stripped Danny down and wrapped him in a sheet. We soaked the sheet with some of our drinking water to try and bring down his fever. I gave him some more anti-inflammatory aspirin and a dose of his pain medicine. I looked at his arm. It was red and swollen and warm to the touch. It was definitely infected. We needed to get this taken care of before he would have to lose his arm.

It wasn't long before the team came back accompanied by a woman. Danny was out of it, so it was just me and them and broken English. The woman's name was Mia Ch'ing, she was a nurse with the local doctor. She and the doctor were both believers. She spoke better English than anyone else in our group. She told me that the police had picked up the doctor and his family after it was discovered that he too was a believer. She was at a patients home when he was grabbed so she was able to escape. She was sure that they had her 2 small children and her husband. When she heard that an American brother was wounded and in need of help, she came out of hiding to see if she could help him.

I ate some food as Mia examined Danny. She said that he would need to be cared for and could not go any further until he had time to heal. She was sure that if she stayed with him and attended to his arm regularly that his arm could be saved. We all talked as we ate flat bread and rice. It was bland but tasted like a little piece of heaven. I was starving! I hadn't eaten in almost 36 hours. As we ate we discussed our plan. One man and I would go and make a new position deeper into the jungle to move our team to. Mia would stay with our other brother to care for Danny and move him into the jungle if need be. The third man would be our look out and sound the alarm if anyone came towards the hide-out.

The brother with me was called Bing. It was a nickname, but it sure made my life easier to call him that. We all gathered around Danny in the cramped space and prayed that God would heal him and that he would not lose his arm. We prayed that God would guide us to a good hide-out that we could move to quickly.

After our prayers, Bing and I left to go search for a new hide-out. We thought it would be best to head out towards where Danny and I had left the motorcycles. There were some good places that had good cover and multiple escape routes. We had been walking for nearly an hour when we heard the sound of a low flying helicopter gunship. Bing was about three yards ahead of me and dived for cover into some thick brush. I leapt to my immediate right and crashed through the underbrush. Instead of hitting the ground and coming to a stop, my body paused and then crashed through the jungle floor. Everything was a blur as my body tumbled and was banged about plummeting to wherever I was falling to. With a dull thud my body hit the ground. It took me a moment to catch my breath as I lay there. I prayed silently to Jesus that if anything was broken that he would heal me immediately. Wow! I hurt. I sat up slowly and looked around. I couldn't see much in the darkness of where I was. I reached into my safari vest and pulled out my faithful L.E.D. penlight. I looked over my body. Aside from some scrapes and bruises there didn't appear to be any major damage. As I looked around, I saw that I had fallen into a deep rocky pit. It was damp and cool in here. I didn't think there was any way I could climb back out the way I came. As I looked around I saw a lot of debris, mostly from when I fell through. I found what appeared to be a hopeful sign of an escape route. I walked over and sure enough, it was. Well, at least it was a tunnel. Lord willing it went somewhere.

I followed the tunnel which was big enough for me to walk in slightly hunched over. It appeared to be a manmade tunnel. Along my underground walk I found several places that widened out into small rooms. At one tunnel junction I found that one tunnel led to a supply room of Vietnam War era supplies. There were old American military meals known as C-rations. Also there were what appeared to be rodent eaten bags that used to have dried rice in them. I found many barrels of water. They were probably no longer good to drink but the barrels would be useful. I quickly took inventory of what was there and continued on to the tunnel junction. I still needed to find a way out and locate Bing. I continued along what appeared to be the main tunnel guessing that it had to lead to somewhere. Sure enough it did, I came out in a hidden entrance just on the outskirts of the very village we fled from. I traversed around the village until I came to the hide-out where Danny and Mia were. I surprised them when I came back alone, but soon explained what had happened. We sent our brother out to the location I described so that he could prepare it for the rest of us. Tonight after the sun set we would carry Danny over there on a stretcher. Meanwhile, I left again in search of Bing.

It took me a couple of hours to locate Bing. He had stopped looking for me when he discovered the pit I had fallen into. He said he figured that there was a tunnel and that I was alright. He said he saw no blood or my body. He continued on looking for hide-outs and things that could be useful. Quickly we got back to our old hide-out. Night was falling and we needed to get Danny moved while it was still light enough to see but dark enough to give us cover.

We got settled into the new place rather easily. That night we decided that Danny would stay in the new hide-out and would receive medical attention from Mia. When he was strong enough and his wound healed, he would return to Cambodia. Tomorrow, I would explain how everything worked for the radio transmitter and the pre-programmed solar powered receivers. Afterwards, I would retrieve one of the motorcycles and head for the border. If Jesus was willing, I would make it there before nightfall and be back in Cambodia. I would probably have to leave the motorcycle in Vietnam, but at least in Cambodia I was not a wanted man.

After much planning and discussion we had a meal of cold rice and warm water. It wasn't much, but it would sustain our bodies. As we all sat around the small candle light in our new shelter, I could not help but think how wonderful God was to provide us with this place. Truly he was the God that heard and answered our prayers. I began to sing "Amazing Grace" softly to God and myself. It wasn't long before Mia and the other three brothers joined in also. What started out as a reflection of God's love and provision, turned into a worship service. They continued singing many songs of praise in Vietnamese and I praised Jesus in spirit and in words of praise.

I slept peacefully that night. It was like there were no problems. No Dark Prince searching to destroy me, no worries about being trapped in a foreign land. You would have thought I was back on *The Messenger* all safe and sound tucked into my own bunk. Not lying on a damp cave floor in Vietnam. God is good.

After a breakfast of cold rice and warm water, we set to work. Over and over I demonstrated the use of the transmitter. With the help of Mia, they were able to understand what I was saying as I explained how it could be moved easily from car to car. The most important part was the small device that had to be attached to the metal body of the car. This would allow the car itself to be the transmitting antenna. It was a pretty simple device to use as long as it was installed correctly.

After Mia reassured me that Danny would be okay and be safely returned to Cambodia, it was time for me to leave. I searched through the old C-rations to find a couple that looked like they were still in good shape and placed them into my small backpack. It was now empty because I was leaving all the receivers and the transmitter here. I was searching for one that contained pound cake. I hadn't had it since I was a boy at hunting camp with my dad. It was the best pound cake I ever had. At least that was the way I remembered it. Hopefully it would still taste good.

We decided that since this was not just a matter of me making it to the border, that Bing should travel with me. He understood the culture and knew many trails and roads along the way. Also, he spoke enough English that we would be able to communicate. This sounded good to me, because the only thing I knew to do was to head straight west through the jungle until I ran into Cambodia.

As the whole group gathered together, kneeling so that Danny too could be a part of the circle; we all took hands and began to pray. As each of us took a turn, my heart began to swell with joy. I wanted to jump up and down praising God. Mia and Bing both prayed in Vietnamese and English. We prayed for each other and for Danny's healing. They each prayed blessings and prosperity over *The Messenger* and her crew. Danny and I prayed for the church here in Vietnam, that through this persecution the Glory of God would be seen and the Saints would be filled with power and courage. In the end, it was hard to tell whether it was a prayer service or a worship service. But really, the two go hand in hand. When worship and prayer are intermingled, they strengthen one another and draw everyone participating closer to God.

With some sadness, Bing and I packed our small amount of gear and headed for the motorcycles. I had only been here in this village for a little more than 24 hours, yet we each felt connected. They would be remembered often in my prayers. I knew there was a good chance that before I was to see them again, most of them would have attained the crown of martyrdom. Although one need not run foolishly into harm's way, martyrdom for Christ was the greatest of all things to achieve as a kingdom man. We had not heard a single helicopter all day, nor did we hear any combat motorcycles as we walked back to where Danny and I had stashed ours. In fact, the jungle seemed to be a peace. This was a great relief to me. I was not looking forward to a long trip back to Cambodia and not really knowing where I was going. It was going to be hard enough without us dodging the government police.

The motorcycles were right where Danny and I had left them. They seemed to be undisturbed. We began to remove the old leaves and brush that Danny and I had covered them with, that were now wilted and dying. As we finished removing the old brush, Bing looked at me with great joy in his face. It unnerved me as his eyes seemed to glow with a light that was unnatural for a man. I was overwhelmed at the sense of peace and love that seemed to be coming from him. "Dear brother," he said, "be not afraid, today I will be at peace and the hand of Jesus will be seen by my own eyes. Be filled with courage and know that you will be unharmed in your travel. No weapon will touch you and no hand will endure against you. Be courageous brother for the Lord has annointed you in this time and you shall carry his message further."

Occasionally I have had someone speak a God-said word to me before, but never like this and never in the middle of the jungle while we were playing hide and seek with the agents of the Dark Prince. It stunned me. He paused over his motorcycle for a moment and drew out his laminated topographical map in its protective sleeve on his gas tank. He then turned around with that same look, and handed his map to me. Then he pushed his motorcycle forward. I stood there slack-jawed for a moment holding the map. I was wondering why in the world he would give me his map when I already had one on my motorcycle. I was about to ask him but he just kept walking away from me pushing his motorcycle. I looked down at the map in my hand. I saw a small red "x" drawn over a spot near the Cambodian border. I looked up to ask Bing what that was about and what in the world was going on. He was about 100 feet in front of me straddling his trail bike. He was twisted around looking at me with his helmet off and he just smiled. It was more than a happy smile; then he turned around and placed his foot on the kick-starter. I was about to yell to him and ask what was this all about, when there was a blinding flash and something hit my body and sent me flying backwards.

I lay there on my back on the ground for a long moment. I was dazed trying to comprehend what had just happened. Suddenly my mind was flooded with an overload of thoughts. The Dark Prince had fired on us. Immediately that was thrown out, there were no other explosions. If his people were firing on us, then there would have been more then one explosion. Unless of course, they thought I was dead also, than they would be here soon to verify the kill. Instantly it hit me! Bing had exploded! I watched him. He pressed down on the kick-starter and exploded. Booby-trap! Bing knew it somehow. As I sat up cautiously, I replayed the whole scene across my mind's eye again. He gave me a prophetic word and encouraged me. The Lord spoke through Bing to tell me that I would be okay and that no one would hurt me. Bing had to know he was about to die and he pushed the motorcycle away from me before he started it. He handed me the map that he marked. I froze. The map! He marked it, now I understood. "X" marks the spot! That "x" is my exit point.

I jumped up as quickly as I could. I realized instantly that I was going to be really sore. I franticly searched for the map that used to be in my hand. Within moments I found it lying beside what used to be a part of an engine cylinder. Again I was dazed for a moment as I looked around at the carnage that surrounded me. There were motorcycle parts everywhere. There was at least one tree that was shredded and scattered. My gaze was fixed on the wreckage while I bent down to get the map. There was no point in even looking for Bing. There is no way he could have survived that and his body would be in pieces. I retrieved my helmet and my motorcycle. Instead of just picking up my trail bike, I knelt down beside it to examine it. If his was booby-trapped, odds were mine was also.

My bike lay on its side, the kick-starter in the ground. From the angle it was laying and the angle I was looking, it took me no time at all to find the crude but very effective bomb. There was a small glass jar taped to the bottom of the gas tank. It was tucked into a little factory groove for the frame rail. Fortunately for me, it was now broken. Someone had taken the spark plug out of the engine and put it through the hole they had made in the lid on the jar. It seemed to be sealed with used chewing gum or something similar. I had seen this kind of bomb before. I first read about it in a book that we used to be able to get in America, but the book was now banned. You would be called a terrorist just by owning such a book and placed in a secret prison by the new Home Land Security forces. Whether they knew it or not, they were a part of the Dark Princes forces.

The government police had simply put a small amount of gas in the bottom of the jar and when an electrical charge was applied to the spark plug, it caused an explosion. When this small bomb went off strapped to the gas tank of Bing's motorcycle, it became a bomb on two wheels. As soon as Bing hit the kick-starter, he didn't have a chance. Had he started his bike next to me, we would have both been dead.

I inspected my motorcycle very carefully. Other than that one alteration, everything seemed to be okay. I didn't appear to suffer any damage from the blast. I set the bike upright on its kick-stand and knelt down beside it to pray. After I finished praising God for protecting me and thanking him that He would allow me to meet such a brave and wonderful man as Bing, I studied my map. I wasn't going to get on the road and I sure wasn't going to take a trail. I had to go cross country. I needed to find a way that the bike could get through to the red "x". After a few moments of study I said a silent prayer and kicked the kick-starter. The bike fired on the second kick. I gunned the throttle and sped off in the direction I had determined.

After several hours of picking my way through the jungle, I came to the only road I had elected to traverse. If I went north on this road for about five miles, I could turn due west into the jungle and be at the "x" in less than a mile. This stretch of road was far removed from any marked city or village so I figured that there was probably no normal police road-block. There wasn't much traffic on this dirt road. Of course, at this time, I wasn't too concerned with regular civilian traffic. I just wanted to avoid the government police.

I traveled down the road and as I came upon the bend where I would turn off into the jungle about one half mile from its center, my heart stopped in my throat. It was a road block. I didn't know if it was normal, or if it was for me, but there it was. I realized I had started to slow down, so I brought the throttle back up to where it was and said a silent prayer. I came as close as I dared and then unexpectedly swerved off the road and into the jungle. There was some yelling and then gunshots. The metallic ring of the AK-47's tore up the jungle behind me as I raced my motorcycle as fast as I could through the brush. Leaves smacked me in the face; small branches broke against my helmet and cheeks. Praise God for goggles or I would have been blind by now. I couldn't hear anything over the whine of my dirt bike as I raced for my destination. I was pretty sure that they would be following me if they weren't already; there were two combat bikes at the road-block.

Suddenly I locked up both brakes on the motorcycle! The ground ended. I slid to a stop only to find that I was at a bluff overlooking a massive river. I looked up and down the river only to see a bridge about a

half mile upstream. I looked at the map.
Had I come to the wrong spot? I looked and I
was right on the red "x". "No way" I shouted!
I got to ride off the edge of this? I was sure
that this had to be wrong. I looked at the
map again. Then I heard the whine of my
pursuers. This was it. I said a loud prayer
to Jesus as I kicked it in gear and goosed the
throttle. I spun the bike around toward the
oncoming motorcycles. Soon I could see
them and I worked my brakes, throttle and
shifter, while slamming my right foot straight
down on the ground. In an instant the bike
did a 180 degree turn and I popped the
clutch and off I went. I was headed straight
for the bluff edge as fast as I could go. Just
before my front wheel was about to go off the
edge, I pulled up with all I had. As soon as I
was airborne, I pushed myself up and to the
side of the motorcycle with every ounce of
strength I had. I wanted to be as far away
from that motorcycle as I could when I hit
that water. When my body was clear of the
bike, I pinched my nose, closed my eyes and
hugged my knees to my chest as hard as I
could. I took a deep breath and waited. I
didn't have to wait long when the sudden
impact on my back and butt hit me. All I

could think of was, "I wonder how deep this water is?"

CHAPTER 5

SAILING AWAY!

In the movies, everything always looks so much easier. In real life, it's much harder. As soon as I hit the water, I realized that I should have taken off my helmet before I hit the water. The force of my impact into the water caused the helmet straps to pull up with such force that I thought for a moment that I broke my neck. At least with me balled up like I was, it minimized the impact on the motor cross helmet. I fumbled with the strap and shed my helmet while underwater. Immediately, my Marine Corps training kicked in. I straightened my body out and hunched my head downward. This allowed the air trapped in my lungs to act as a balloon and gently lift my body upwards to the surface. I just relaxed and went along for the ride. My lungs were burning when I finally broke through the surface. Immediately, I flung my head back and released the air in my lungs and took a new breath. Air felt good! I began to swim when I saw a small boat drifting with the current and a man waving at me. I swam to the boat and the Vietnamese man helped me aboard.

I rolled over on my back and looked up. There on the bluff edge that I had just ridden my motorcycle off of, were the four men who were pursuing me. I couldn't help but sit up and wave at them. One of them waved back. I started to laugh hysterically. I wonder if he realized how ridiculous that seemed. They had just been trying to kill me.

The boatman steered for the shore. As we pulled alongside a makeshift bamboo dock, I reached into my safari vest and pulled out a soaking wet roll of American bills. I handed him a wet twenty dollar bill and said thank you as I bowed. With that, I leapt off the boat onto the dock. I headed past all the little boat equipment stands, fish shops and other assorted things here at the dock and headed for the nearest place I could find to hire a car and get back to the orphanage. The sooner I was out of Cambodia and into the Philippines, the better I would feel. I did need to stop and explain to Danny's family and let them know where he was and all that had happened. The events of the last couple days were swirling through my head as I struggled to unpack every thought.

I found a car that would carry me to my destination just outside of Phnom Penh, the capital of Cambodia. When I got there, I rented an inexpensive hotel room. I needed to grab some rest, a shower and shave. I also wanted to get my clothing laundered. I had been in the same clothes for a few days and aside from my recent swim in the river, I hadn't been able to get clean since I set out for Vietnam. I thought about just calling Danny's wife, but thought that that would be a very poor thing to do. Honor as a kingdom man required me to always carry this kind of news in person. True there were times when this could not be done, but most of the time we find it hard to go out of our way for people. Being a kingdom person requires us to have a heart that cares about people and goes out of our way to demonstrate that heart of caring. It is not a part of our lifestyle if we just say we believe something, we must exercise it for it to be a part of us.

After a fine dinner, a good night of rest, and a hearty breakfast, I checked out of the hotel and headed for the orphanage. I put my ear-buds in and was surprised to find that my mp3 player still worked after all the abuse it had recently suffered. I sat in the back of my hired car and worshiped Jesus, my wonderful friend and protector who always cares for me. I had about a two hour car ride so I could really just relax and pray and worship.

As the car pulled to a stop in front of the orphan compound, I turned off my mp3 player and handed the driver fifty dollars in American money. The bill was forty dollars, but God calls us to be a blessing at all times, so when I have it, I tip heavily.

I walked slowly through the compound gate. I wasn't sure how to best tell Danny's wife the situation. I knew everything would be okay, but she wasn't there and she was his wife. She would think of things differently than I would.

She came hurriedly across the grounds when she saw me. Quickly her face changed to a worried questioning look. I knew in a moment that she realized that he wasn't with me. She came right up to me, and asked "Is he alive?" "Yes" I said gently. "Is he in prison?" she asked me. "No," I answered, "he is safe and will be home soon." She seemed to relax noticeably when I said that. I said that we should gather the elders and teachers and meet in the church so that I could share. She agreed and sent their housekeeper to gather everyone together at the compound church in an hour. She walked with me to the church as she asked me her most pressing questions. I told her briefly about the box cutter wound and being chased. I explained about his wound festering and God providing a nurse and friends and the underground hide-out. She was praising God as we sat alone in the church. We prayed together for Danny and his safe return and quick healing. We were finishing up our prayers when people started coming in.

I stood at the pulpit with Danny's wife next to me to translate for me. I explained in great detail everything that had happened.

After that we began to worship and praise God. We took turns praying for the church in Vietnam, Mia and our brothers who were still there to continue the fight against the Dark Prince and his forces in Vietnam. We prayed for Danny and the others who were wounded in this persecution. We prayed also for Vietnam and that the Glory of God would be seen there.

I was hoping to leave for the dock and my ride out of the country after stopping by the orphanage, but our impromptu service went on for many hours. Afterwards, the women went to prepare a meal for all of us. Danny's wife demanded that I stay the night and rest under their roof and in the morning one of the men would take me to the docks. There was no way I could say no. I was glad to have the warmth of such a large family tonight. Reliving the last couple days also brought back many painful memories and there was great sorrow in my heart for the men and women that had been lost while I was there in Vietnam. God tells us to rejoice in our hardships for they bring us discipline. Obviously he didn't mean to rejoice when terrible things happen. He means to rejoice in the growth that and maturity that comes as a kingdom man or woman. Kept in perspective, death for us and the hardships of this life are only a fleeting time for us. We grow and become greater kingdom soldiers and then we pass from death into life everlasting with the King of kings; Jesus.

I lay in my well-worn cot praying to and praising Jesus. I don't know when I fell asleep, but I woke up about 5 am. The sun was just about to break over the horizon when I got out of bed and went outside to sit. As I watched the sun burst through the night, I could not help but declare how great God is in His creation.

I had breakfast and coffee with everyone. So many people came to lay hands on me and pray. Finally through tears and hugs we all parted ways and I left for the docks. This place in Cambodia would remain dear to me for all of my days.

My driver helped me find my contacts; Tom and Patty Pence. A retired couple from England who owned a 60 foot ketch named *Pearl of Love*. They were a sweet couple who just resonated with the joy of the Lord. They were people that just made you feel warm just to be around.

The *Pearl of Love* was a beautiful ketch. This twin masted sailboat had teak wood floors on top that were called the "deck". Down below (what they called the down stairs) was a large dining area and lounge or living room combined. There was a small but well equipped kitchen and a very large shower and bathroom. The Pences had a large master bedroom in the back of the boat called the "aft". They placed me in the forward bedroom. It had two single beds in it. Because of the layout of the boat, I had my own bathroom and shower. In the middle of the boat was an enclosed pilot house. This was one beautiful boat.

On my first night aboard they insisted on taking me to the best restaurant in town. I tried to politely refuse, but Tom looked at me and said "nonsense! How could you ever refuse, that would be robbing us of an opportunity to be a blessing." With that argument, I had no choice. I went down below to shower and shave and change clothes. I laid out all the clothes I had on my bed to find something that would be suitable for the nicest restaurant in town. What did one wear to a really nice place to eat? I decided on my best pair of khaki colored cargo shorts and a short sleeve button down sportsman shirt. I figured I would leave my safari vest and just carry my wallet and pocket knife and all tool. When I went topside to meet up with the Pences, I was surprised to see Tom in sandals, Bermuda shorts and a tacky tropical short sleeve shirt. Patty came up from below after a few minutes and looked at me and smiled. "You look very nice Johnny." She said. She was dressed in a very nice summer dress with sandals and a scarf around her head like a bandanna. "Thank you Mrs. Pence, you also look very nice." She smiled brightly and replied, "Ignore Tom, he doesn't care how he looks. He loves his tacky tropical shirts. I gave up trying to change him thirty years ago." Now it was Tom's turn to smile. He said, "It was a long hard fight, but in the end I was victorious!" He began to laugh from deep down. You could tell he was a man who loved to laugh.

After a really nice dinner we returned to the *Pearl of Love*. I lay in my bunk enjoying the quiet of this boat. There was a little bit of clanging from a near-by sailboat, some piece of something or other not secured properly. Tom complained about it a few times but it seemed kind of nice to me. The boat gently rolled back and forth and before I knew it I was sound asleep.

Morning came with the smell of bacon cooking. I sat up and almost fell over; the boat was at an odd angle. Almost as if she were falling over. We must have been moving or underway as a sailor likes to say. I stepped out into the dining area and Patty was there at the stove cooking. "Ah there sleepy head, I thought the smell of bacon and coffee would rouse you from the land of the dead," she said with a great big smile on her face. She continued on, "We thought we would let you sleep in until you woke up yourself. You seemed awful tired yesterday evening. I was just fixing breakfast. Are you hungry?"

I realized that I was now starving. I hadn't smelled bacon being cooked since I was last at home in the states. I poured myself a cup of coffee from the thermos that Patty pointed out and sat down at the table. "Thank you, and yes I am hungry now that you mention it," I said.

"Well, go on up to the cockpit pit with Tom and I'll bring it up to you," she said very sweetly.

Upstairs in the covered pilot house I found Tom at the wheel. "She's got an auto-pilot, but I feel better steering her myself" he said while never even turning to see who it was. "Come over here lad while I show you what to do. We have a lot of miles to cover and you can give a hand. Have you ever sailed before?" he asked.

"I have a small pokey cruiser that I've sailed a little." I replied. "She's just a little single masted job, nothing as nice as the *Pearl of Love*."

Tom responded as Patty brought up a tray filled with breakfast up, "This ole' tub isn't much different. Same principle, just a little more work. Do you enjoy sailing your girl? What was her name?"

"The *Kay-T-Did*," I replied with a smile, "and yes, I love to sail her. She is easy to handle and loves to sail."

"Boys," Patty interrupted, "enough talk about your mistresses, it's time to eat. Tom, would you care to thank God and ask His blessing over our meal?"

After breakfast, Tom and I spent the next few hours talking about sailing while he showed me around the *Pearl of Love.* It really wasn't much different than my boat; except a lot bigger and two main sails instead of one.

Just before 2 o'clock in the afternoon Patty yelled up that she had a good satellite video connection with *The Messenger.* So I went downstairs and had a video conference with *The Messenger's* commander, Charlie Johnson. Charlie had given his life to Christ after years of drinking. He was a self-made man, but when he decided to retire at an early age he just spiraled down into addiction. A wonderful man of God, a great kingdom man began picking Charlie up for church every Sunday. If Charlie was drunk or hung over it made no difference. Then came a day when God got ahold of Charlie and he immediately gave his life to Jesus. He devoured the Bible in no time. There was a massive revival going on in that day called the Brownsville revival. Charlie went down there and something happened, he came back a completely different man. He wasn't just in love with Jesus; He was on fire for the Kingdom of God. He traveled all over the world on Christian mission trips. Seeing how things were working for many third world pastors, Charlie began to implement some new programs in the states. He soon moved from his own house into an out building with an outhouse and no electricity or plumbing. He decided that to really get a heart for the people he was ministering to that he needed to live like them. He exhausted his own fortune in several years, but he had built a great kingdom organization. Now years later, Charlie sat at the head of what would in all probability become the hub of communication and logistical supply for the harshest countries that worked in resistance to the Dark Prince.

Charlie asked how things had gone on this operation. He listen very patiently as I explained every detail to him. He asked that I put it into a written report and email it to him. I told him that it would take some time for me to do that.

"Johnny," he said, "the Pences are taking a roundabout way to Hawaii. I want you to go with them. When you get to Hawaii, contact me via internet and I will get you a ticket back home. Spend some time with your family. Just stay in touch with me when you can establish a connection with *The Messenger.* I will let you know when we are steaming back to the states. We will pick you up then. I will probably have you go down to our school and train a few of our new recruits while you wait for us. You did a fine job, I am proud of you son. We have some unexpected things to take care of on our end so we will be delayed and unable to make it to the Philippines as expected. Stay in touch son and may the blessings of Jesus be with you."

With that, he signed off and the briefing was over. I went topside and informed the Pences that it looked like I would be their guest all the way to Hawaii. They were thrilled. Patty went on and on at how much fun this would be.

For the next two weeks we island hopped around the south Pacific. We went to Christmas Island, Borneo, Australia, and many others. I kept back two hundred dollars of the money I had for an emergency reserve, but the rest of the money I gave to Tom to help off-set the expenses of the trip. He complained that it was way too much, but I reminded him that he would be robbing me of a blessing if he didn't take it. We both laughed at that as he handed the money to Patty.

We were out near the Marshall Islands. I was down below about to go to sleep. I had just been on watch for eight hours. It was now midnight and Tom had relieved me. I put my ear buds in for my mp3 player. I had taken to listening to it as I drifted off to sleep every night. This night didn't seem any different than any other night. Drifting off to sleep as the boat sailed gently through the calm south-Pacific was beautiful. Sleep came easy. I had long since stopped being haunted by the death of Bing.

I was jolted awake by the sound of gunfire. I sat there for a second. Did I have a bad dream? Suddenly I heard Patty scream. I raced out of my room and headed for the enclosed pilot house when there was a blinding flash in my head.

When I came too, I was lying on the floor. My hands were tied behind my back and my feet were tied together. There was a rag tied around my mouth to gag me. My head felt as though it were ready to explode. I was having trouble focusing my eyes. With a great deal of effort, I could make out Tom lying next to me. I couldn't see where Patty was. I heard men talking in a strange language. I had heard it before but right now I couldn't place it. I moved my head to try and look around. It hurt so bad I thought it might explode at any time. I finally got a look at the three men standing at the wheel. Pirates! We had been taken by pirates. They looked small and slight yet well-muscled. The best I could do was place them from somewhere around south-east Asia. This wasn't looking good at all. By them keeping us alive meant that it was going to be really bad for us. Normally they just kill the owners when they take a boat. If they were keeping us alive it was because they were going to make money off of us; either in the slave trade or more likely, by cutting out our organs and selling them. Kidneys brought good money on the open market. So did livers and practically everything else inside of us. We would be parted out like a used car.

I began to pray. I prayed for courage and strength. I prayed that God would display his might. I also prayed if God wanted to call me home now that would be good with me, just don't let them cut me apart piece by piece to sell on the market. I asked him to make it a heroic death to glorify his name.

I opened my eyes just in time to see them drag Tom down below. Then one of the men grabbed my legs and started dragging me down below also. They pushed me into the forward cabin where I had been sleeping and closed the door. It was dark and I could feel Tom and someone else that I suspected was Patty. I knew that only God could deliver us. His word says so, and it is His word that I live and die by now. I am a Kingdom man. I serve the Lord Jesus Christ. With that, I began to praise Him out loud. It was muffled because of the gag, but I praised him as loudly as I could. It wasn't long before Tom began to join me in a muffled praise session.

THE END OF

BOOK ONE

Look for the next exciting

Book in the

Adventures of Johnny
McGinnis

Check out other books from Mickey Wilcox.

"THE MOST EXCELLENT WAY"

The true events leading up to and through my personal salvation experience.

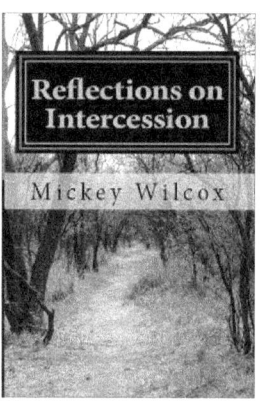

"REFLECTIONS ON INTERCESSION"

Journey with me through my experiences in the awesome power of prayer and Intercession.

All books available on Amazon and my web site:

www.mickeywilcox.org

Follow "**12 Minutes With Mickey**" on
Facebook at
www.facebook.com/mickey.wilcox

Check out my website to learn more of the
exciting ministries God has placed in my life
at:

www.mickeywilcox.org

For questions, speaking engagement
schedule, or
to learn more about this amazing Jesus,
email me at:
usmc_mic@hotmail.com

www.ingramcontent.com/pod-product-compliance
Lightning Source LLC
Chambersburg PA
CBHW070758120626
46557CB00002B/655